Hodder
Children's
Books

a division of Hodder Headline plc

Sophie and the Seawolf

Helen Cresswell
Jason Cockcroft

*Once upon a time there was a girl called Sophie,
and this girl went for a ride on a sea wolf.
You don't have to believe it, but I do.
It's a wild and wicked and tearaway story,
and even if it isn't true, it ought to be.*

It all began with Sophie talking to the sea. She had lived by it all her life and knew its different voices, from the merest whisper to the hollow boom of breakers in a storm. She wasn't exactly sure what it was trying to say but it seemed only polite to talk back.

"Morning sea, morning waves!" she'd yell as she kicked along the ragged fringes. She'd tell it things. "One of my front teeth is coming loose and six sixes are thirty six as a matter of fact!"

Much the sea seemed to care. It slapped up the shingle and tossed little fistfuls of spray against her legs, and it seemed to Sophie that she might as well be talking to herself. "You might be bigger than me and wetter than me but you're certainly not so good at talking!"

*S*he said these things, but secretly she felt in her bones the deep mysteriousness of the sea. And sometimes at night she would look out of her window up at the sky and see millions and millions and millions of stars, and she felt the mysteriousness of those, too. She would even stretch her arms up as if to touch them, though she knew she couldn't. "You can't touch a star and you can't touch a wave," she thought. "That's a funny thing. They're there, all right, but you can't hold them."

And Sophie wanted to hold them. She wanted it with all her might and main. She wanted it so badly that sometimes she felt she might burst.

And, as everyone knows, if you want a thing badly enough, it happens. So when Sophie met the sea wolf, it was almost as if she had wished him out of thin air – out of thin, salt air.

He stood on the tideline, as wolfish a wolf as there has ever been since the world began. His coat was thick and grey, his eyes were yellow and fixed on Sophie as if he had wished her out of air.

There they stood and looked at one another, and Sophie felt her heart go thump thump thump because although she had never met a wolf before in real life, she had in stories. She knew that they went in for frightening little pigs and even gobbling people up. She did not wish to be a wolf's breakfast.

"So you're the one who talks to the sea," the wolf
remarked. "You're the one who talks to the stars."
 "Only some days," said Sophie. "And what's that
to do with you?"

"When you talk to the sea and stars, you talk to me," the wolf replied.

"Well I never knew that!" said Sophie, and she didn't either.

Because the wolf seemed to know her, even if she didn't know him, she edged up a little closer. Now she could see the crusted salt glistening on his coat like frost.

"You had better touch me," the wolf said.

So she did. She touched him gingerly at first, and he was sea-cold, icy. Then she scrunched her fingers into the dense fur and could feel the warmness of him.

"You had better admit that I'm real," he told her. "You were wondering, weren't you?"

"I suppose I was, rather," Sophie said. "I've seen plenty of crabs here before, and jellyfish, but never a wolf."

"I don't expect your mother lets you go out at night?" he said.

"Oh no," she said. "Never."

"You'll never learn anything if you don't go out at night," he told her. "Meet me here when the church clock strikes twelve."

"Twelve midnight?"

"Twelve midnight. Do you promise?"

"I promise," said Sophie.

By a quarter to twelve, her mother and father were fast asleep and her baby brother lay sucking his thumb where the moon made patterns on his quilt.

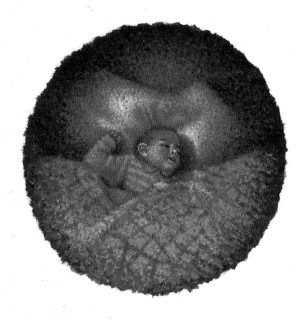

Sophie stole down the stairs and through the quiet house, and turned the key in the back door and was outside.

The moon shone broad and white and the air was colder than daytime air. Sophie sniffed. The smell was curiously green and icy.

She started to run towards the harbour. As she reached it, the church clock began to strike the hour and the wolf was there. His coat was frosted and his eyes gleamed silver.

"You can keep a promise, then," he said. "Climb on my back."

"You might run off with me, " said Sophie.

He smiled a wolfish smile and for the first time she saw his pointed teeth. Then he lifted his head and howled, and at the sound, little cold prickles ran down Sophie's spine. Perhaps there was no such thing as a friendly wolf.

"Climb on my back," he said again. The whole
world seemed to hold its breath. Should she
go with that dangerous enticing wolf or stay with
her feet safe on the ground? She stuck out her
chin and made up her mind.

He stood quite still as she threw an arm round
his neck. She could feel and smell the salt in his
rough coat, and now she was looking down at his
sharp wolf's ears. She remembered, rather late, the
story of the gingerbread man.

"By the way, I'm not made of gingerbread," she said, then, "wheeeee!"

Because the wolf was running, he was stretched to twice his length and Sophie's hair streamed out behind her and the cold air filled her mouth. He raced away from the harbour and past the church and its crowded graveyard with tombs and crosses bleached by the moon.

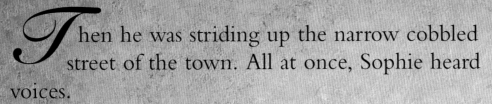

$\mathcal{T}$hen he was striding up the narrow cobbled street of the town. All at once, Sophie heard voices.

"No! No! Come back, Sophie!"

She looked up and saw that the whole town must have been woken by the wolf's howl, as if it were cockcrow or the last trump. Windows were flung open and there were pale faces with dark holes for mouths as they screamed.

"No! No! Come back, Sophie!"

But Sophie wouldn't and couldn't and now – aaah! – with one last stride he was up up up and airborne. The wolf was running in the air as if it were his element, he went easily, easily skimming the roofs and chimneys.

"No! No! You'll never come back, Sophie!"
The voices faded as the wolf went climbing the cold
invisible path towards the stars. He was going his own way
and nothing could stop him. And Sophie was going with him,
like it or not.

She looked down and saw how tiny her town was now.
Then she looked up and saw that the moon and stars
were rushing to meet her, and all the time the only sound
was the pant of the wolf's breath over his shoulder.

"He's running off with me and I might never come back!"
thought Sophie, but she did not care. She even took one
of her arms from round the wolf's neck to see if she could
touch a star.

Then, suddenly, she was in a storm
of gulls, their wings flashing in a navy sky.
She had always wondered where they went at night,
and now she knew. They dipped and soared and
screamed as if the air were crammed with invisible
fish, and so it might have been for all she knew.

Sophie didn't know anything any more.
The whole world had changed in the
twinkling of an eye. The wolf had done it.
He had picked her out and dared her.

"I dare! I dare!"

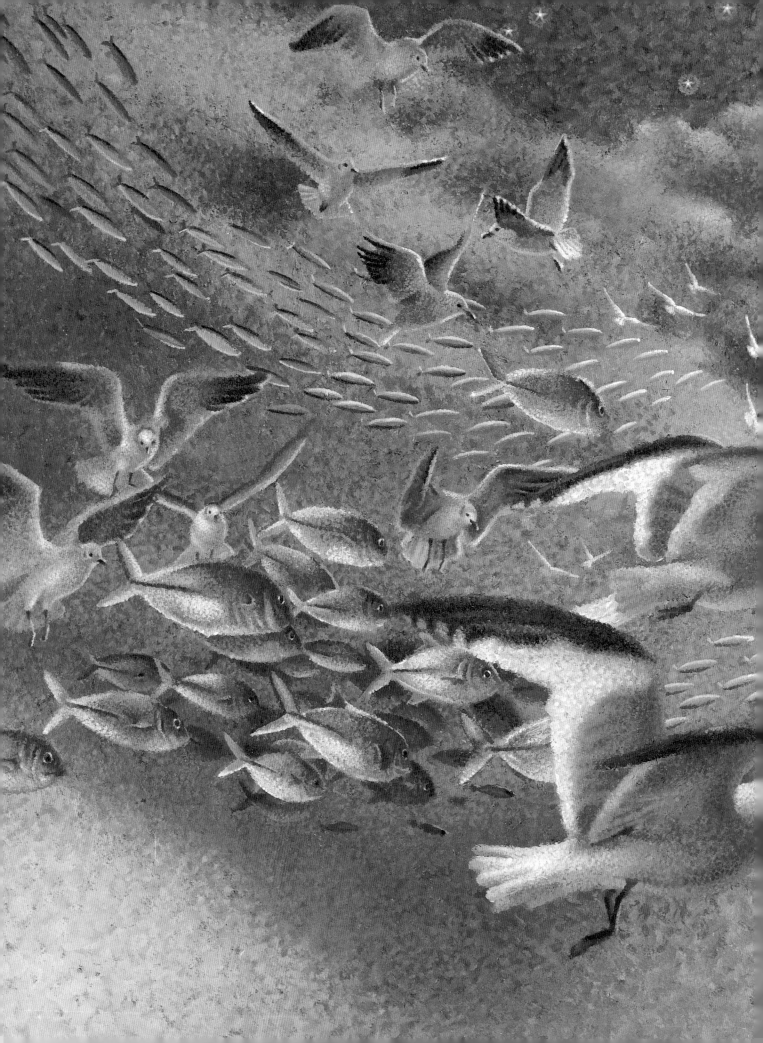

When she looked down again, they were over
the waves, and by now she was not sure
whether the sky was full of fish and the sea full of stars.
She was riding the air on a wolf's back, and if that was
possible, so was anything, anything at all.

"*H*urray, wolf!" she cried, and
hugged his strong neck
and wanted to stay there forever. But
he had turned and ahead and down
below she could see the crowded roofs
of her little town all painted silver, and
the pale ribbon of the sands.

Then she heard voices, blown by
the wind.

"Look! There! There they are!"
The wolf went striding down
and touched the sand again with a
little soft thud. He stood motionless
and Sophie climbed down and stood
there, dizzy and suddenly cold.

"Sophie! Sophie!" the voices clamoured.
"Well?" said the wolf. "What will you do?"

Sophie stared into his silvery eyes and knew that she loved him and wanted to be with him forever.

Then she looked up the beach and saw the people: men, women and children all in their night clothes, tall and white like ghosts. She saw her mother and father and baby brother and made up her mind.

"I'll stay, wolf," she said.

And she knew, without him saying a word, that she would never see him again.

"Remember me," he said.

Then he was running again, stretched to twice his length, and a gasp went up from the crowd as he started to rise, treading the air, going seaward, moonward.

Then the people started to cheer because the wolf had gone and left Sophie safe on the shore. But tears went sliding down Sophie's cheeks. She had gone with the sea wolf into a wild world and now she was safe home. He could not stay and she could not go, and that was the end of that.

But once you have been for a night ride on a sea wolf, you are never the same again. Sophie wasn't. For one thing, she wanted the whole world to see what she had seen.

As a matter of fact, she told me this story – and now I'm telling you.

Just in case you ever meet a sea wolf.